S0-DMX-120

HIS FINEST HOUR

David Neuhaus

Viking Kestrel

VIKING KESTREL
Viking Penguin Inc., 40 West 23rd Street, New York, New York 10010, U.S.A.
Penguin Books Ltd, Harmondsworth, Middlesex, England
Penguin Books Australia Ltd, Ringwood, Victoria, Australia
Penguin Books Canada Limited, 2801 John Street, Markham, Ontario, Canada L3R 1B4
Penguin Books (N.Z.) Ltd, 182–190 Wairau Road, Auckland 10, New Zealand

First Edition

First published in 1984 by Viking Penguin Inc.
Published simultaneously in Canada
Printed in U.S.A.
1 2 3 4 5 88 87 86 85 84

Library of Congress Cataloging in Publication Data
Neuhaus, David. His finest hour.
Summary: Ralph, hoping to impress the local bicycle racing team, uses his secret rocket engine in a race against his friend Dudley, but afterwards only Dudley is asked to join the team.
[1. Bicycle racing—Fiction. 2. Sportsmanship—Fiction] I. Title.
PZ7.N4427Hi 1984 [E] 83-23547 ISBN 0-670-37260-9

For Mom, Dad, Janet, and Pat

Special thanks to
James Marshall

This is Dudley.

This is Dudley's friend Ralph.

TEAM SAW
GUISEPPE DRINKS MILK
THE NEW EXQUISITO

Dudley and Ralph have been friends for a long time, although sometimes Ralph doesn't play fair.

One day after school, Ralph saw his heroes, the local bicycle racing team, speed by. He dreamed of being asked to join the team, and he thought of a good way to show off. He challenged Dudley to a bicycle race.

WILBUR LLOYD WRIGHT
SCHOOL
7

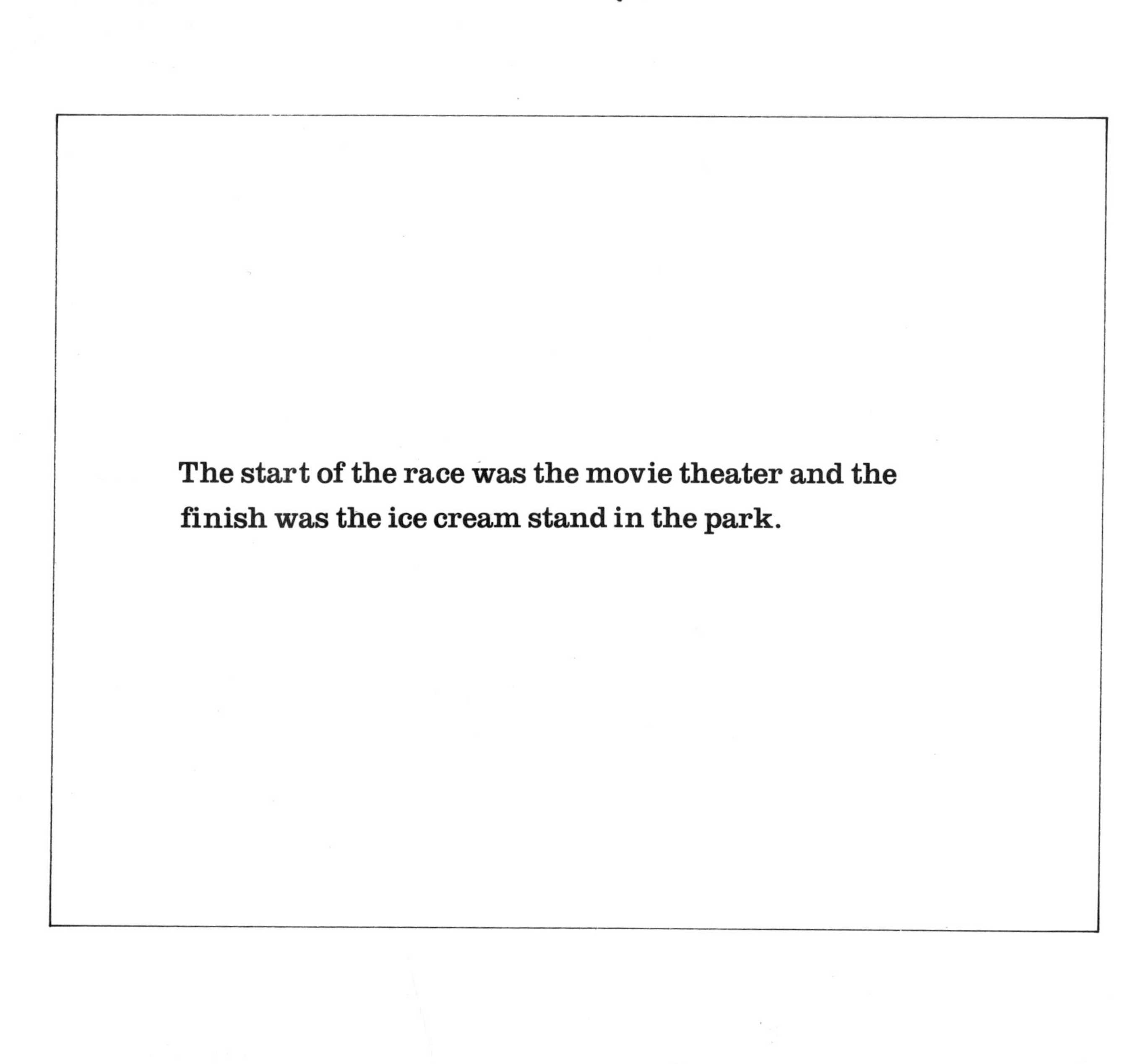

The start of the race was the movie theater and the finish was the ice cream stand in the park.

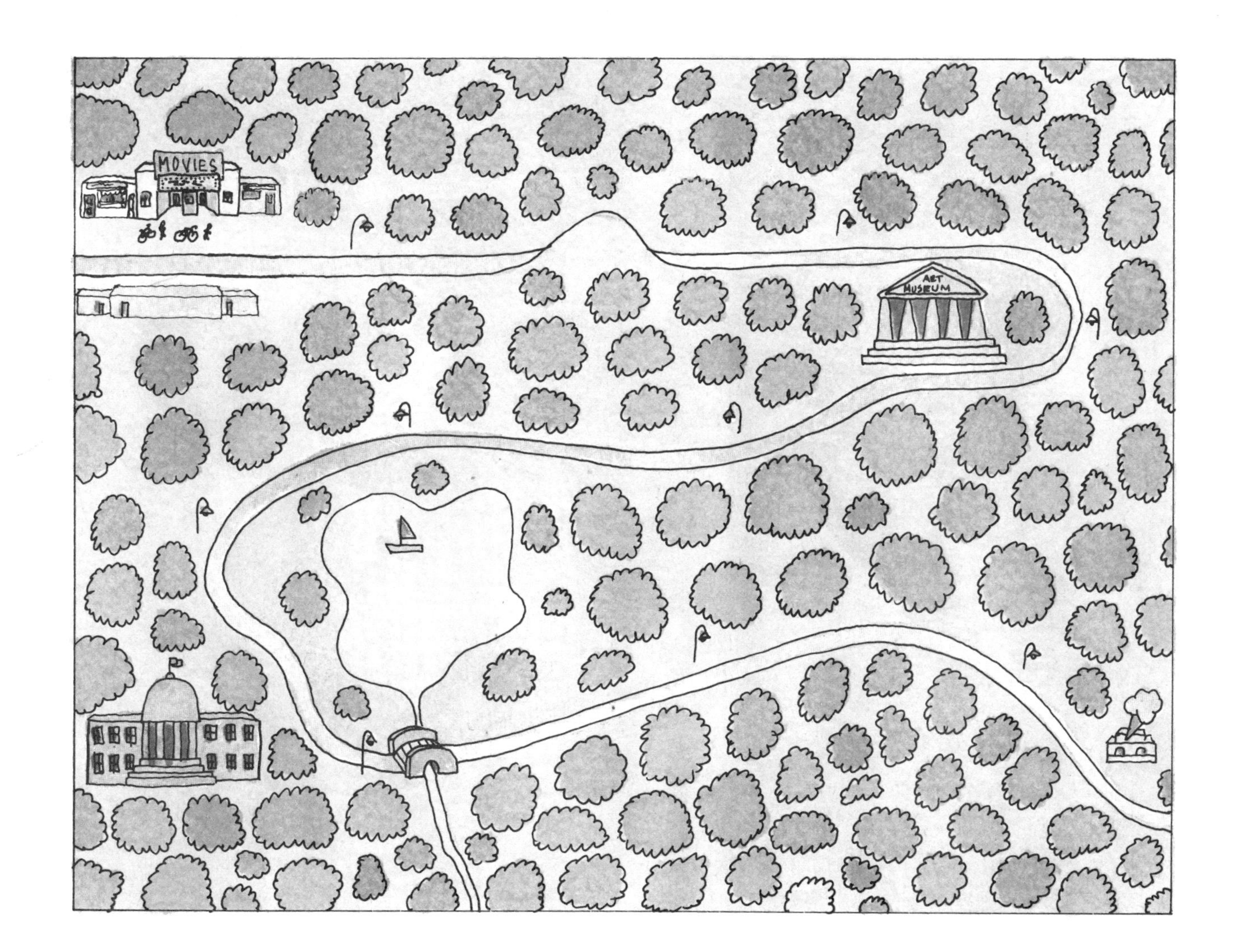
MOVIES
ART
MUSEUM

Ralph arrived at the starting line with his bike, leather biking shoes, deerskin gloves, silk shirt, nylon shorts, embroidered cap, high-pressure pump, imported tools, and water bottle filled with a special fruit juice for extra energy.

Dudley came with his bike.

MOVIE
WHATEVER HAPPENED TO UNCLE FRED
Sparky's BARBER SHOP
OPEN
SOON

When the starting gun was fired, Ralph shifted gears
and took off like a bullet.

OVIE
R HAPPENED
LE FRED
PHARMACIST
Rx
BICYCLES
MAR
SALE
LEMON
Substitute

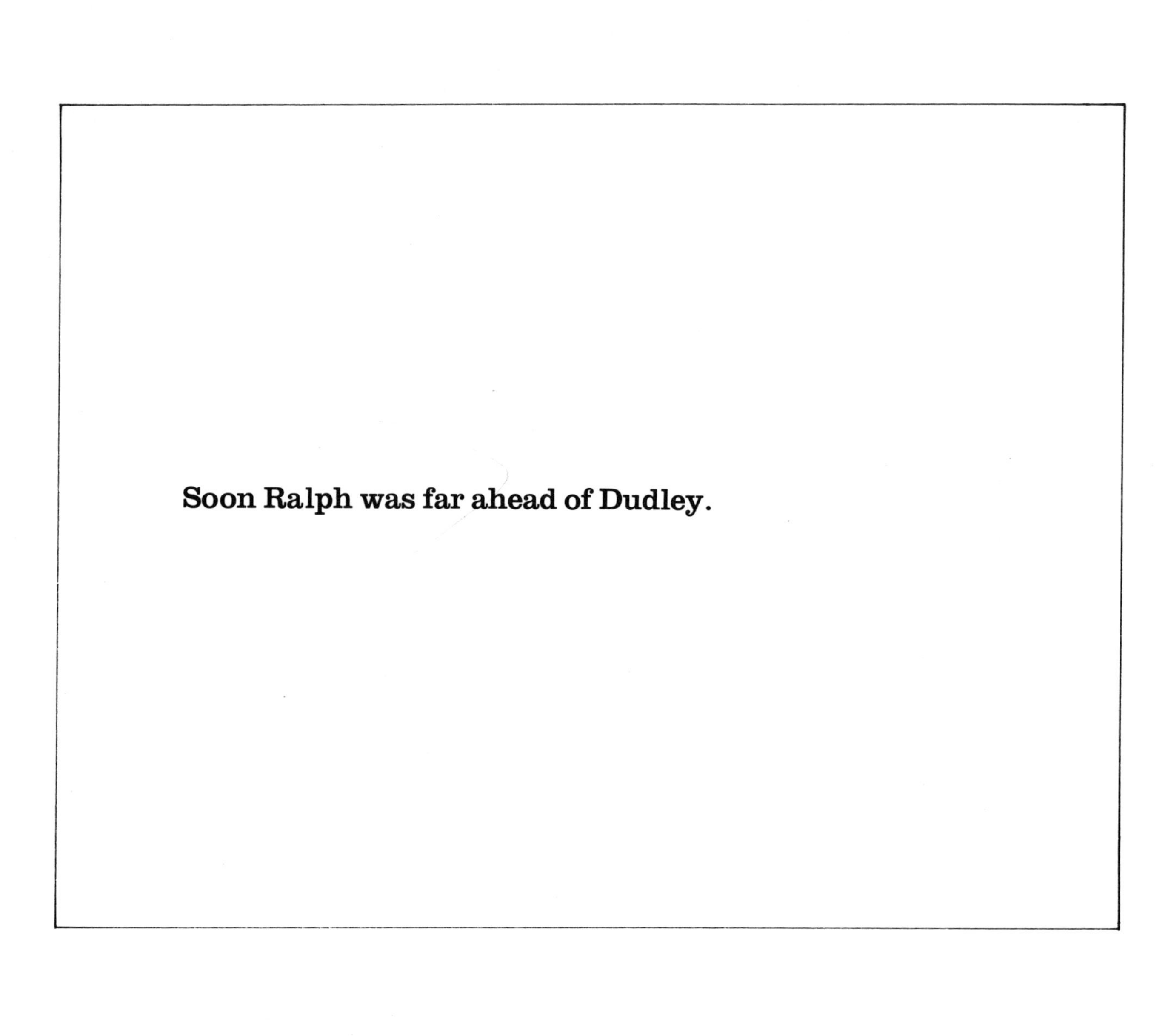

Soon Ralph was far ahead of Dudley.

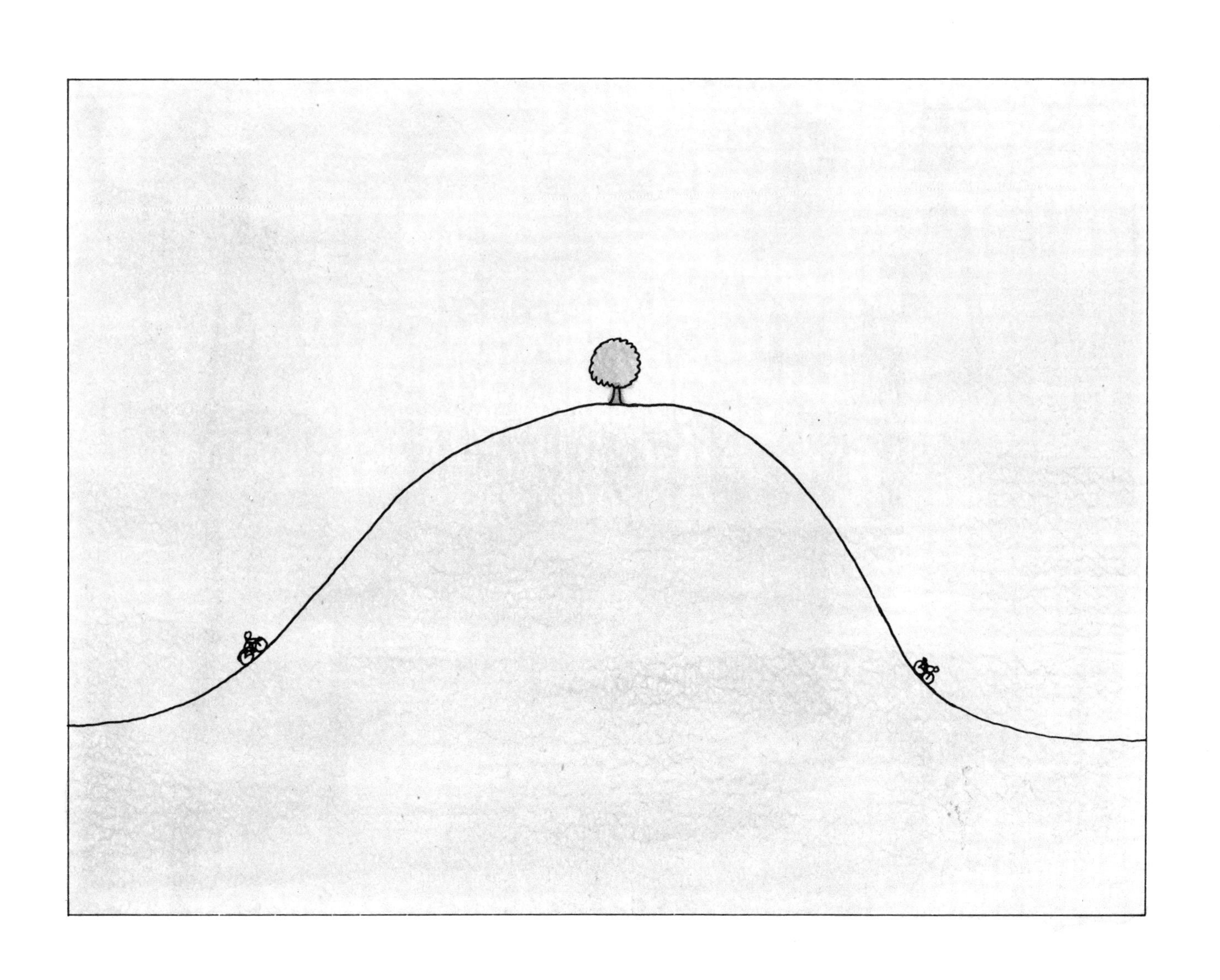

Ralph saw some pretty girls sitting on a park bench. He decided to show off.

Dudley pedaled on. From out of nowhere, the racing team appeared and shouted words of encouragement.

When Ralph realized that Dudley had taken the lead, he decided to use his secret weapon, and he switched on his rocket engine. Whoosh went the engine. Zoom went the bike.

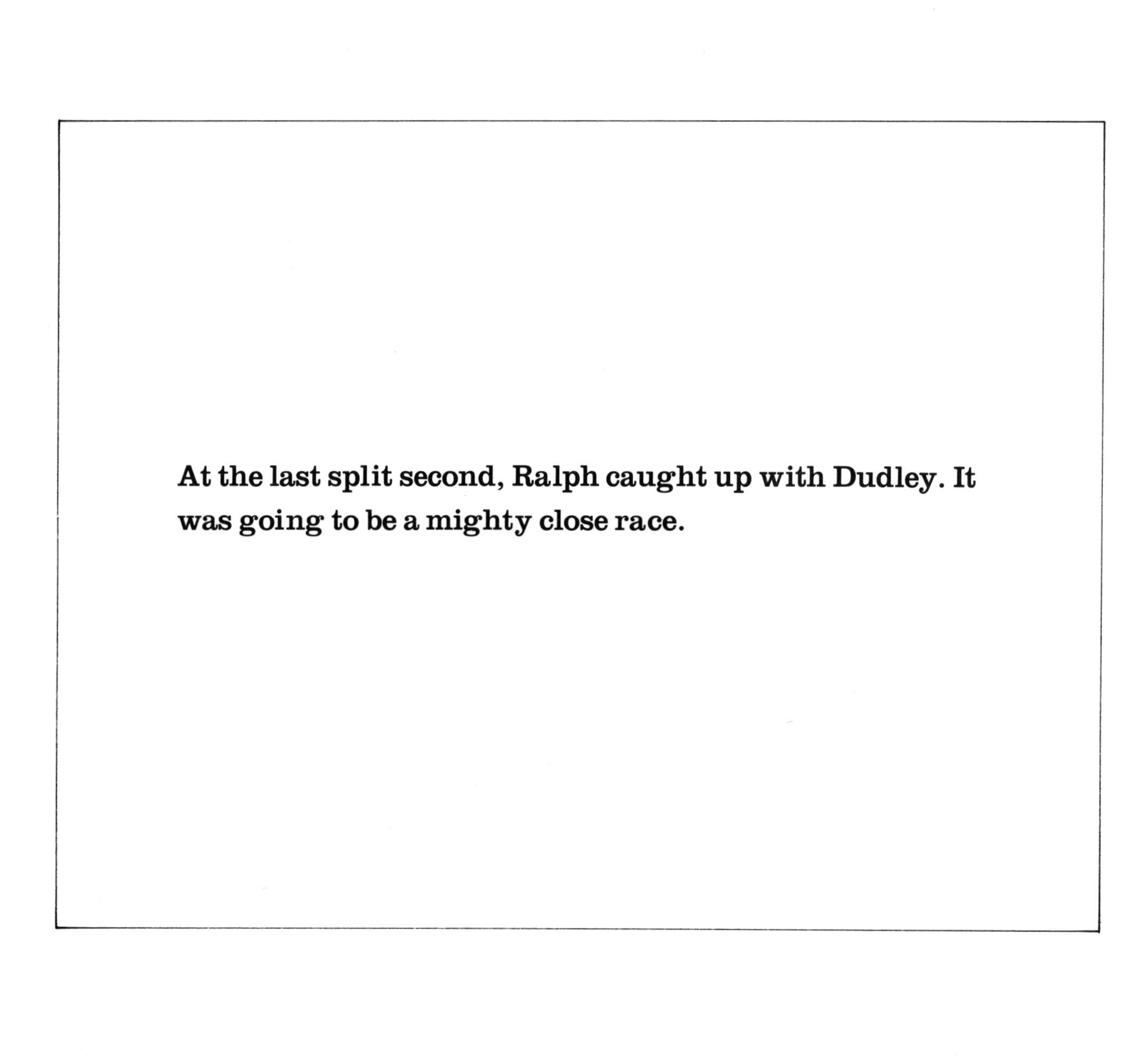

At the last split second, Ralph caught up with Dudley. It was going to be a mighty close race.

Ralph beat Dudley by half an inch.

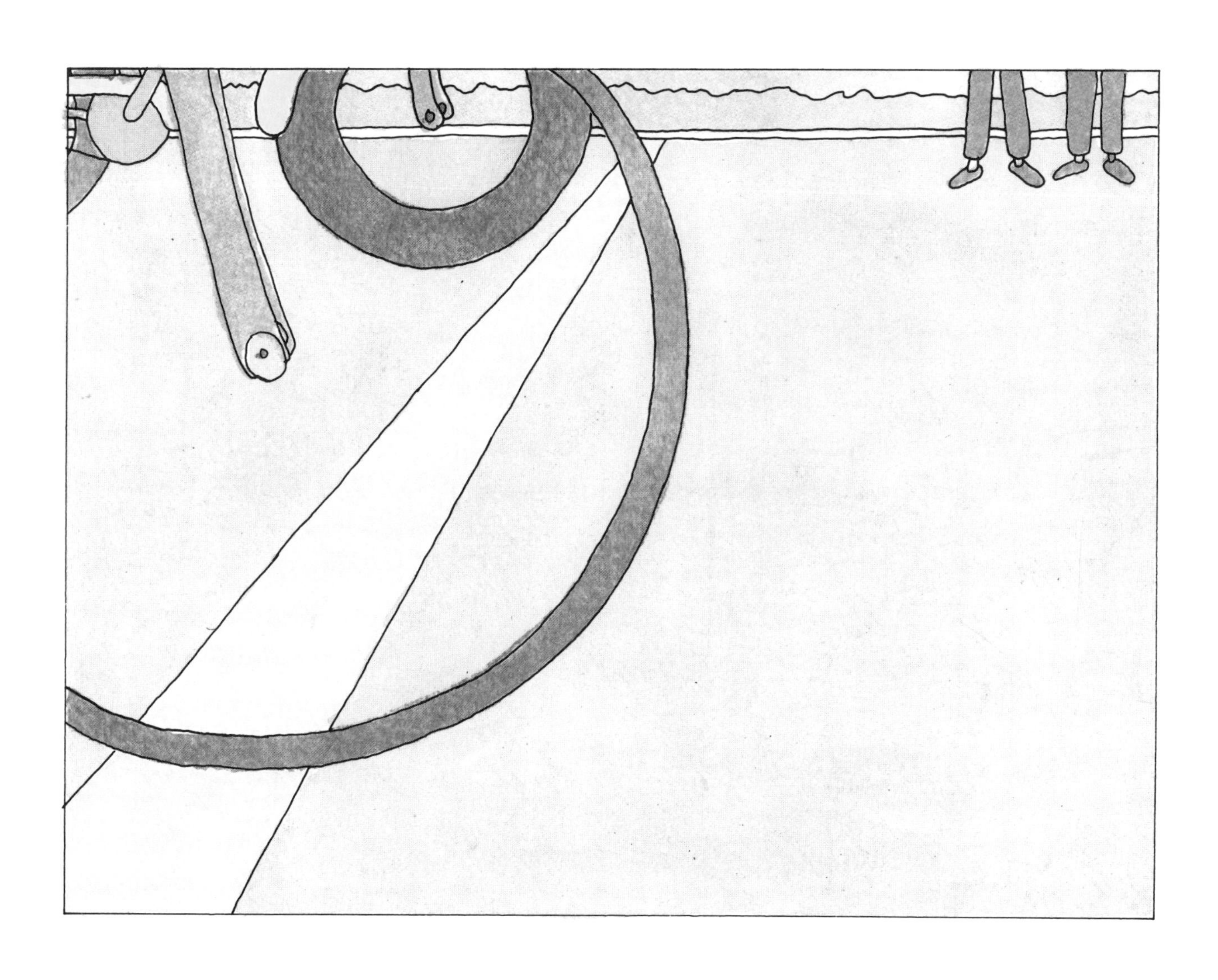

The crowd applauded Dudley's good sportsmanship and the team captain asked him to join the team. Then the captain treated everybody to ice cream cones. Everybody except Ralph, who couldn't be found.

ICE
CREAM

Ralph hoped that his rocket engine would soon run out of fuel.